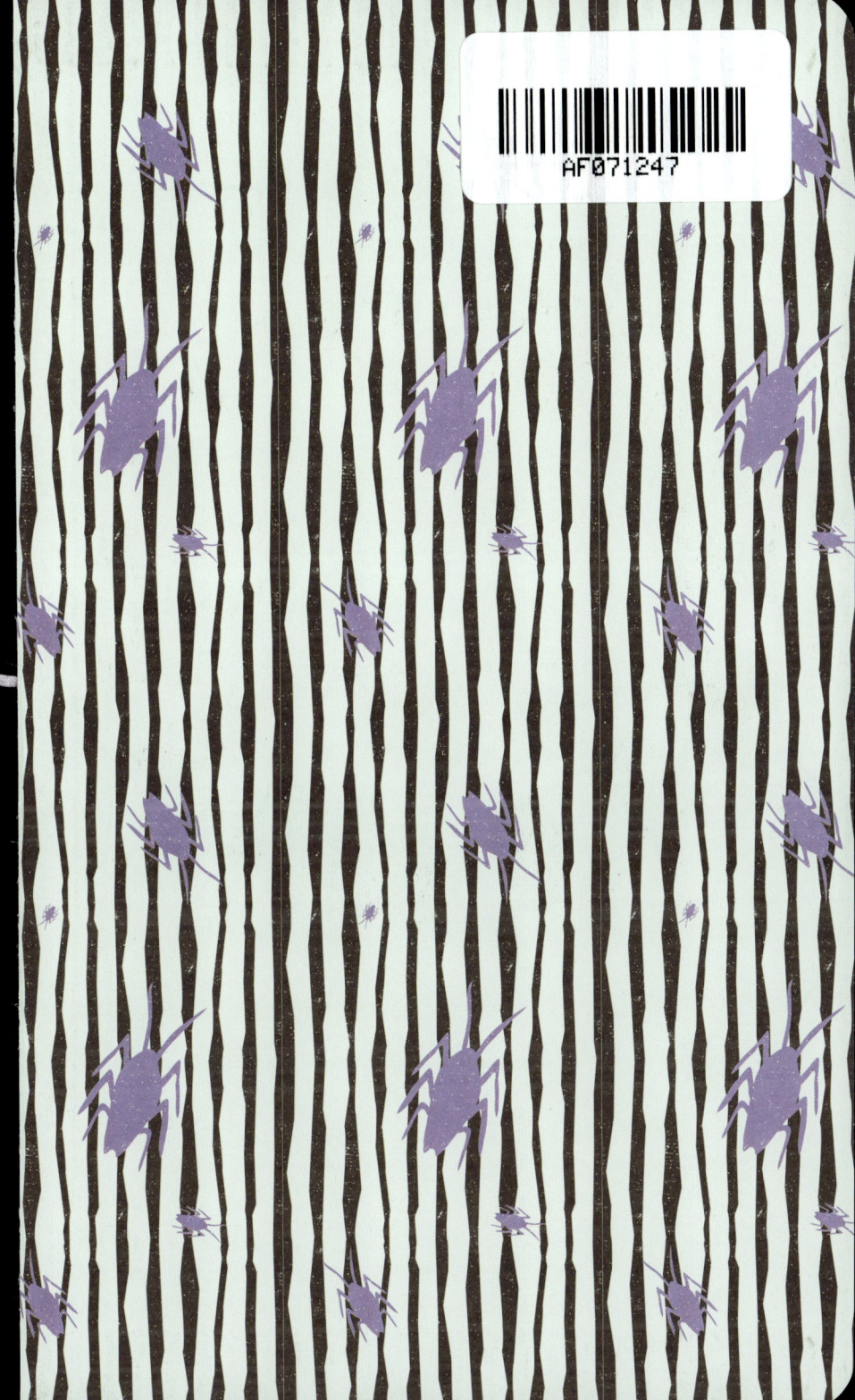

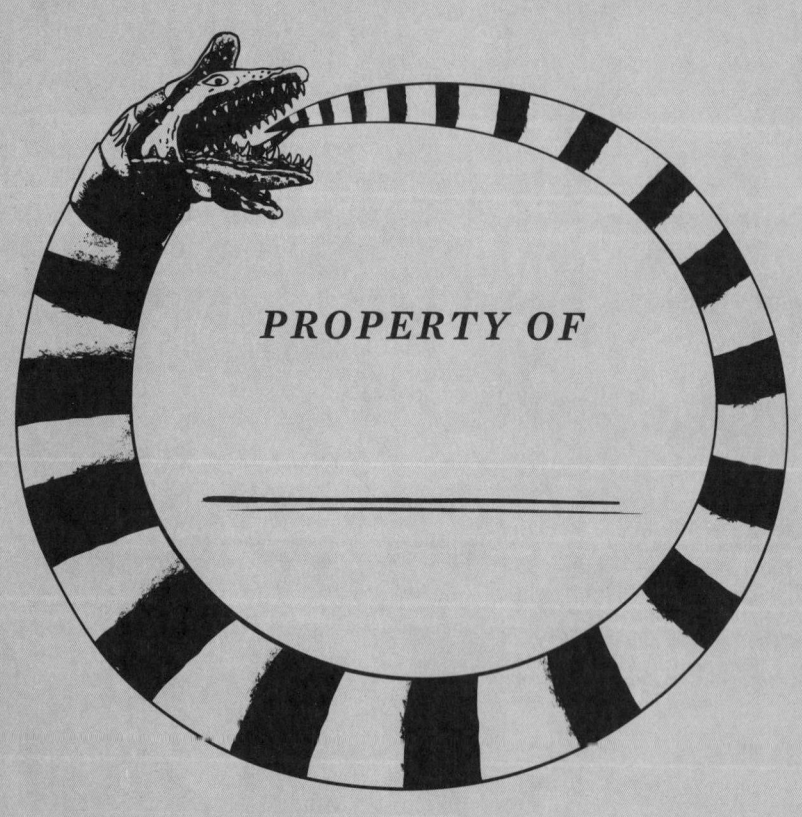

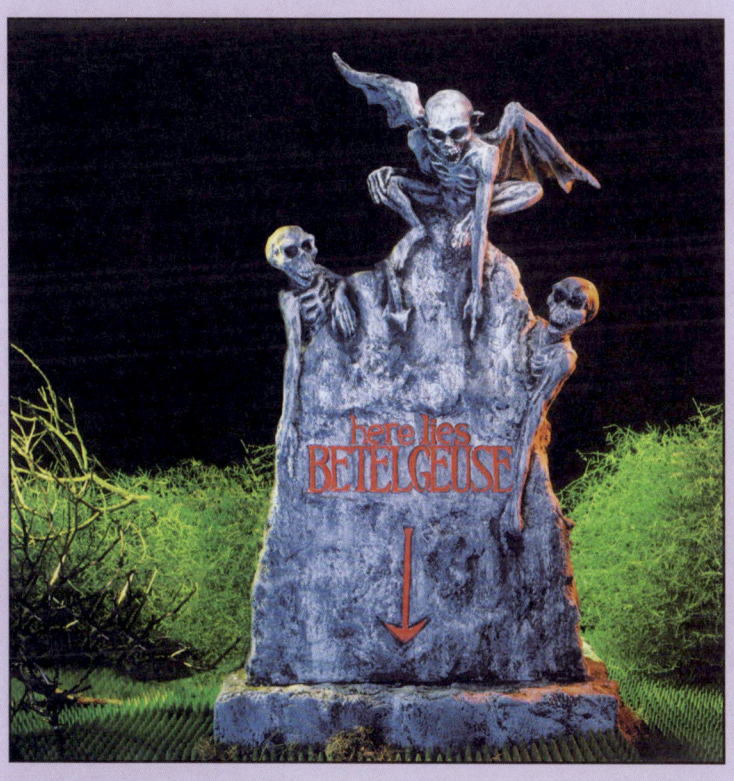

BEETLEJUICE™

BEETLEJUICE and all related characters and elements are
© & ™ Warner Bros. Entertainment Inc. (s18)

INSIGHTS

an imprint of

INSIGHT EDITIONS

www.insighteditions.com

MANUFACTURED IN CHINA
20 19 18 17 16 15 14 13 12 11

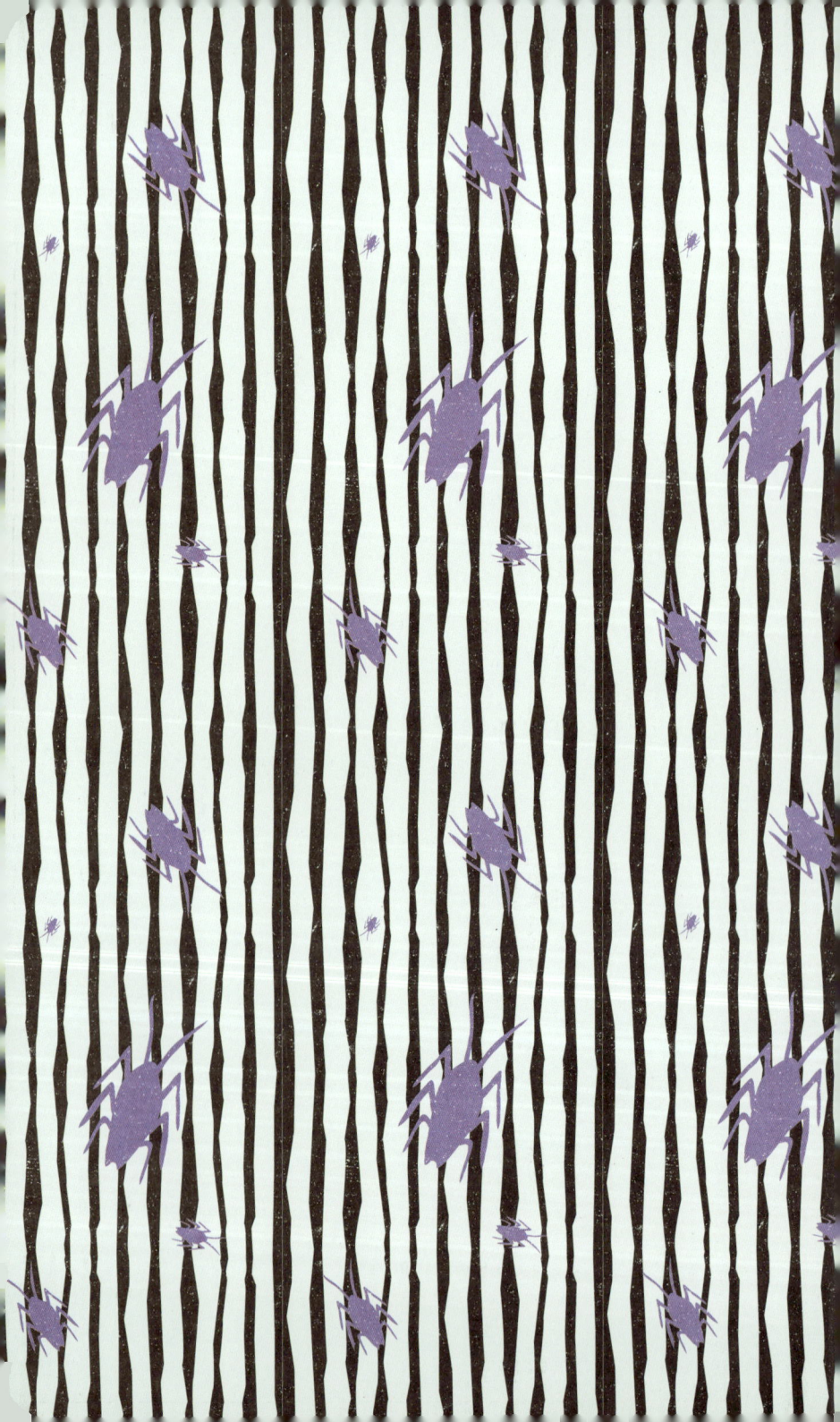